Edmund and Washable

CHRIS JACKSON

A TALE FROM
CHINA PLATE FARM

 HarperCollins*Publishers*Ltd

To my Dad ~
the one and only

EDMUND AND WASHABLE
Copyright © 2000 by Chris Jackson.
All rights reserved.
No part of this book may be used or repro-
duced in any manner whatsoever without
prior written permission except in the case of
brief quotations embodied in reviews.
For information address HarperCollins
Publishers Ltd, 55 Avenue Road, Suite 2900,
Toronto, Ontario, Canada M5R 3L2.

http://www.harpercanada.com

HarperCollins books may be purchased for
educational, business, or sales promotional
use. For information please write:
Special Markets Department, HarperCollins
Canada, 55 Avenue Road, Suite 2900,
Toronto, Ontario, Canada M5R 3L2.

First HarperCollins hardcover ed.
ISBN 0-00-224558-2
First HarperCollins trade paper ed.
ISBN 0-00-648534-0

Canadian Cataloguing in Publication Data

Jackson, Chris, 1953–
Edmund and Washable

ISBN 0-00-224558-2

I. Title.

PS8569.A2525E35 2000   jC813'.54
C99-932410-1
PZ7.J33Ed 2000

00 01 02 03 04 05 Acorn 6 5 4 3 2 1

Printed and bound in Hong Kong/China

On a crisp autumn day, Edmund sniffed the air that blew around China Plate Farm and knew it was apple time. He made his way cheerfully down to the orchard. There would be windfall apples in the lush grass beneath the trees.

He nosed through the grass looking for the
first hint of red. But instead of apple red,
he found pink. Pig pink.

"Oh, boy!" thought Edmund. "Wait 'til
Hillary sees this!"

"Hillary, look what I found! His name's Washable—it says so right here on this label. See?"

"Oh, well done, Edmund!" exclaimed Hillary. "You've found it! The girl child will be so happy to have her toy back."

"Her toy?" asked Edmund.

"Yes, Edmund. 'Washable,' as you call him, belongs to the girl child staying at the farmhouse. You weren't thinking of keeping him, were you?"

WASHABLE

"Why not?" asked Edmund indignantly. "What's that saying I've heard around the farm, something about *finding tweezers…?*"

"*Finders keepers, losers weepers?*"

"Exactly," said Edmund. "Now if you'll excuse me, Hillary, I must show Washable his new home."

Edmund was stopped in his tracks by an amble of cows heading for the dairy.

"Good morning," said one of the cows. "What's all the rush?"

"Good morning, madam," Edmund replied. "This is Washable. He will be staying with me from now on."

"But, Edmund," said the cow, "isn't that the girl child's toy?"

"Well, *find the keys and lose the peas*," Edmund said. "Or something like that."

A knot of sheep blocked the gate.

"Hey, Edmund," a sheep called out. "What's that you've got there?"

"It's Washable. He's a pig—looks like me—same colour—needs to see his sty—sorry, have to go."

"But, Edmund, isn't that the toy we saw the girl child with the other day?" the sheep asked.

"As Hillary says," Edmund replied, "*remind the sheepers to wear their sleepers.*"

Next Edmund met a wobble of ducks and geese.

"Good morning, Edmund. Is that the girl child's toy you've got there?"

"Let's get this straight," said Edmund in a rather short manner. "His name is Washable. He's not a toy, he's my friend, okay?"

"Well, whatever it is, we're glad you found it. The girl child will be so pleased to have it back."

"Oh, no. I'm not giving him back. He's mine now. After all," said Edmund, "you know what they say— *jeepers creepers, ducks and geesers.*" And with that he disappeared into his sty.

"What is it with everyone?" Edmund complained to Washable. "The cows can have friends by the herd, sheep have friends by the flock, and geese have them by the gaggle. But have one more pig on the farm and everyone gets upset. Why can't *I* have a friend just like me?"

Later, as it began to get dark, Edmund heard noises outside and got up to investigate. There were people in the orchard with flashlights. The farmer was on his hands and knees in the tall grass. The girl child stood nearby. The farmer stood up after a while and put his arms around the girl child's shaking shoulders and led her back towards the farmhouse.

"Well, *finders keepers*," Edmund said defiantly to himself. But as he drifted into an uneasy sleep, a thin little voice added: "*Losers weepers, losers weepers…*"

Edmund had a dream that night, the worst dream a mud-loving pig could have: he dreamt he was sitting in a huge tub of warm soapy water.

"Hey!" yelled Edmund. "I'm not washable!"

Looking up, he saw Hillary and the rest of his friends standing at the edge of the tub. They all looked very sad.

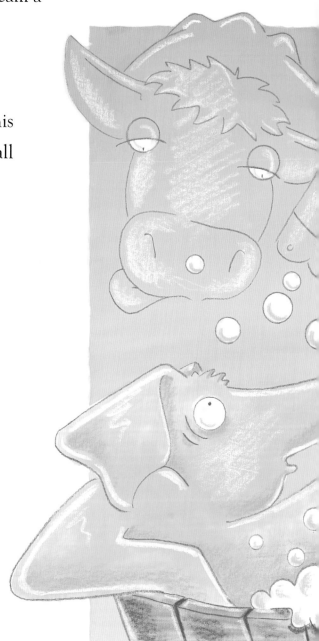

"I miss Edmund so much," said Hillary.

"Yes, we all do," agreed the sheep.

"But the girl child did find him," said the cows.

"And if she found Edmund, then she gets to keep him," said the geese. *"Finders keepers."*

"Still, we have Washable here," said Hillary. "Do you think he's clean enough now?"

"But I'm not Washable!" shouted Edmund.

He awoke with a start and knew immediately what he must do.

The following day, under the trees in the orchard, Edmund waited while the girl child poured juice into tea cups. She handed out snacks on plates to all her guests. Edmund enjoyed the apples, but remembered it would be bad manners to eat them all.

When the picnic was over, the girl child collected her toys, including Washable, and gave Edmund the biggest of big hugs.

"Found a new friend?" asked Hillary.

"Oh, you mean Washable," said Edmund. "Well, actually, I gave him back."

"No," said Hillary. "I meant the girl child. You know, it's just like you said: *finders returners, friendship earners.*"

"I said that?" asked Edmund.

"It was something like that," said Hillary.